I0689416

COME AS YOU ARE

BY MM MYERS

BROKEN

LOVED

REDEEMED

ISBN 979-8-9922064-1-8 (paperback)
Copyright © 2025 by MM Myers & Firestorm publishing LLC. All rights reserved.
This book is protected under international copyright laws. No part of this publication may be reproduced, distributed, or transmitted in any form or by any means, including photocopying, recording, or other electronic or mechanical methods, without the prior written permission of the copyright owner, except in the case of brief quotations embodied in critical reviews or articles.

Unauthorized reproduction or distribution of this book is strictly prohibited and may result in legal action. If you wish to use any part of this book for educational or non-commercial purposes, please contact Firestorm Publishing LLC for permission.

Thank you for respecting the hard work and creativity that went into this book!

Firestorm publishing LLC
Of Moore, Tx

DEDICATION

To my children and grandchildren,
whose laughter and wonder have been my greatest inspiration.
You are the spark that keeps my stories alive and the reason I even try to write.

To my dear friends and family, and some very special ladies such as Cece Johnson, Helen Crow, Linda McGinnis, Claudia Sturdevant, Jodie Keith, Sheila Ball, and Teresa Leister—
Your unwavering support and encouragement have meant the world to me. Thank you for believing in me and inspiring me to keep sharing my stories

With much love, MM Myers

To God be the glory

About This Storyteller

In a world where words often flow effortlessly, I have found my voice through the timeless art of storytelling. I consider myself more of a storyteller than an author—perhaps because "author" feels too formal for the simple yet heartfelt tales I weave. Each story I craft carries the warmth of laughter and imagination, shaped with care and love.

My journey as a storyteller has not been without its challenges. As someone who is legally blind and has navigated the complexities of dyslexia, reading aloud in my younger years was often a daunting task. Yet, these obstacles never extinguished my passion for storytelling. Instead, they deepened my appreciation for the spoken word, allowing me to create vivid worlds and vibrant characters that spark the imaginations of my listeners and bring joy to their hearts.

As a mother, I cherished the magical moments spent sharing stories with my children—their giggles and wide-eyed wonder were a constant source of inspiration. Later, as a grandmother, I realized the importance of preserving these stories. Much like my own grandmother's cherished tales, I wanted to ensure that these memories would not fade with time. My grandchildren became my muses, inspiring me to transform my spoken words into written ones.

Though the process of writing is far more challenging than simply telling a story, I embrace it wholeheartedly. Each imperfect sentence is a reflection of my journey—one fueled by love, laughter, and the desire to keep our family's legacy alive. My hope is to capture the same excitement I see in children's eyes and share that joy with readers of all ages, preserving the magic of storytelling for generations to come.

MM MYERS, Storyteller

Come As You Are

Prologue

Marie pressed her back against the cold, damp wall of the basement, her knees drawn tightly to her chest. The faint light from a single, flickering bulb above barely illuminated the bruises on her arms. She willed herself not to cry—tears only made her mother angrier. Better to sit in silence, hidden in the shadows, as she had learned to do long ago.

The house above her groaned in the night, the creak of floorboards a reminder that her mother was still awake, pacing, muttering curses under her breath. Marie shuddered as she thought of the words she'd heard over and over again: "You're nothing but a burden. A mistake. A demon."

But tonight, something was different. In the suffocating darkness, a whisper reached her ears. It wasn't her mother's voice. It was gentle, steady, and warm.

"I love you. I died for you."
Marie froze, her heart pounding. She strained to hear more, but the voice was gone, swallowed by the silence. She shook her head, thinking she must have imagined it. Yet, deep in her chest, something she hadn't felt in years: hope.

The next morning, she climbed the stairs cautiously, every muscle in her body tense, ready to dodge another blow. Her mother's voice was sharp and cutting, but Marie didn't linger to hear the rest. She slipped out of the house, her feet carrying her down streets she didn't recognize, her hands trembling with each step.

When she stopped, she found herself staring at a small church. Its doors were open, and the sound of a hymn floated out, soft and inviting. She hesitated. Her torn clothes and disheveled hair were like a banner announcing her brokenness. What if they told her to leave?

But the whisper returned, more certain this time.

"Come as you are."

Marie stepped inside.

CHAPTER 1: SHADOWS IN THE BASEMENT

Marie's tiny frame trembled as she curled up on the cold, unforgiving concrete of the basement floor. Her knees pressed tightly to her chest; arms wrapped around herself as if to shield from the world above. The air smelled of mildew and damp earth, clinging to her skin like a second layer of grime. The darkness was oppressive, swallowing everything around her, except for the soft, warm bodies of the dogs who had crept close, their fur brushing against her tear-streaked cheeks.

Her mother's voice still echoed in her ears, sharp and venomous: "Shut up, or

I'll give you something to cry about!" Those words were a blade, cutting into her heart every time they were spoken. She had tried—oh, how she had tried—to stifle her sobs after being hurled down the basement steps, but the pain of her fall and the ache in her heart were too much to contain. Her cries had betrayed her, spilling out into the suffocating silence.

And then the light had gone out.

The door had slammed shut.
The lock had clicked into place, sealing her in the darkness.

Marie buried her face into the fur of the scruffy mutt who had come to her side, his tail wagging faintly as if to say, "I'm here. I won't leave you." The dogs were her only friends in this house, her only solace. She clung to them now, her fingers gripping tightly to their coats as her body shook with silent sobs.

Why does she hate me so much? The question burned in her mind, a constant refrain she could never silence. She had asked herself about this every day for as long as she could remember. At seven years old, she had already learned that love was not something guaranteed—not for her, at least. Her older sister, Clara, got smiles and hugs. Her baby brother, Tommy, was cradled and cooed over, his every giggle met with laughter and affection. But Marie? Marie got the glares, the harsh words, the blows.

She didn't understand.

She had tried so hard—so hard—to be good. She stayed out of her mother's way. She did her chores quietly, hoping that if she scrubbed the floor just a little harder, or folded the laundry just a little neater, maybe her mother would see her. Really see her. But no matter what she did, her mother's eyes always seemed to burn with contempt every time they landed on her.

There were times when Marie would catch her mother staring at her with a look that was almost… haunted. As if Marie was some kind of ghost, something that shouldn't exist. And then the anger would come, oh the anger …. fierce and unrelenting, and Marie would find herself back here, in the basement, with the bruises blooming on her skin and the dogs as her only comfort.

She sniffled, wiping her nose on the sleeve of her tattered dress. Her voice was a broken whisper as she spoke to the dogs.

"What did I do wrong?" she asked them, her words trembling. "Why does she hate me? I didn't mean to be bad. I didn't mean to make her mad."

The dogs tilted their heads, their eyes glinting softly in the darkness. They didn't have answers, but their presence was enough to keep her from feeling completely alone.

Marie's thoughts drifted back to the few memories she had of her father. He had been gone for years now, but she could still remember the way he used to lift her up onto his shoulders, making her laugh as he spun her around. Back then, her mother had been different—softer, kinder. But after he left, everything had changed. Her mother's smiles disappeared, replaced by a permanent scowl. And Marie... Marie had become the target of her mother's rage.

It was almost as if her mother blamed her for his absence. Or even his very being!

Marie didn't know why. She didn't understand. But she felt the weight of that blame every day, pressing down on her like an iron chain.

The sound of footsteps overhead snapped her out of her thoughts. She tensed, her body going rigid as she listened. Her mother was pacing back and forth, her voice muffled but angry. Marie couldn't make out the words, but she knew that tone. It was the tone her mother used when she was on the verge of exploding.

Marie held her breath, her heart pounding in her chest. She prayed that her mother wouldn't come back down here, that she would let her stay in the basement with the dogs. At least down here, in the darkness, she was safe from her mother's hands.

The footsteps faded, and Marie exhaled shakily. She rested her head against the dog's side, her fingers stroking his fur as she tried to calm herself.

Maybe tomorrow will be better, she thought, though she didn't really believe it. She had been telling herself that for years now, and tomorrow was always the same.

But still, she clung to the hope, fragile as it was.

Because hope was all she had.

CHAPTER 2: THE TARGET CHILD

Marie always knew she was different. Not because of anything she had done, but because of how the world around her treated her. The term "target child" didn't exist in her seven-year-old vocabulary, but she lived it every day. It was an invisible mark, a label she couldn't shake, etched onto her existence by the person who was supposed to love her most: her mother.

Marie watched as her older sister, Clara, basked in the sunlight of their mother's affection. Clara was the golden child, the one who could do no wrong. Clara claimed the room that they shared as her own with soft pink curtains and shelves lined with dolls that Marie wasn't allowed to touch. Clara got new dresses for every school year and holidays, ones with bright patterns and lace collars, while Marie wore only hand-me-downs that were too big for her small frame, for Marie was very tiny too tiny really.

And then there was Tommy, her baby brother. He was the apple of everyone's eye, the child her mother and stepfather doted on endlessly. Tommy's laughter filled the house like music, his chubby hands reaching out to be held, his every cry answered with comforting coos. Tommy was her stepfather's pride and joy, the son he had always wanted.

Marie, on the other hand, was invisible to them—or worse, a burden for This is how she felt for the last few years.

Her stepfather, though kind to her, was often too distracted by work and Tommy to notice the bruises that Marie tried to hide. He was the only one who treated her with gentle words, who asked her how her day was or gave her an occasional pat on the head. When he was home, the house felt different. Safer. Her mother's anger seemed to evaporate in his presence, as if his kindness had the power to keep the storm at bay.

But when he was gone, the storm always came back.

Marie didn't understand why she was the one her mother hated. She had spent countless nights lying awake, staring at the ceiling, trying to figure it out. Was it the way she looked? The way she spoke. Was it because her real father had left? She didn't remember much about him—just fragments of a memory, like the way he used to call her "pumpkin" or how his laughter would fill the room.

But he was gone, and her mother had remarried, and now it was as if Marie's existence was nothing more than a reminder of something broken.
Her mother's words echoed in her mind constantly:

"You're useless. A mistake. Nothing but trouble."

The words stung more than the blows. They stayed with her, burrowing deep into her heart until she began to believe them.

Marie learned early on how to survive. She stayed quiet when Clara bragged about her new toys. She stayed out of sight when Tommy was being cuddled and kissed. She did her chores without being asked, hoping they might win her some small scrap of approval. But no matter what she did, it was never enough. She was never enough, nor could she be good enough...

The Church on the Corner

It was a Sunday morning when Marie first discovered the church. She wasn't supposed to leave the house—her mother had made that clear—but something about the way the sunlight streamed through her bedroom window that morning made her feel bold. She slipped out of the back door and wandered down the street, her feet carrying her toward the sound of singing.

The church was small, with peeling white paint and a steeple that leaned just slightly to the left. The doors were open, and inside she could hear voices raised in harmony. Curious, she stepped inside, her heart pounding in her chest.

The room was filled with people, their faces alight with joy as they sang. Marie slipped into a pew at the back, unnoticed, and listened. The words of the song washed over her, unfamiliar but somehow comforting.

Amazing grace! How sweet the sound,
  That saved a wretch; like me!
I once was lost, but now I am found,
  Was blind, but now I see.
'Twas grace that taught my heart to fear,

And grace my fears relieved.
……. The music was so, Marie didn't
know but she felt she needed to hear at
this moment in time… so beautiful yes
that's what the music was she had never
heard anything like it before but before
she knew it there on her cheek were tears
and she didn't even know why!

The music continued……

When we've been there ten thousand
years,
   Bright shining as the sun,
We've no less days to sing God's praise
   Than when we first begun.
For the first time in her life, Marie felt…
seen. Not by the people around her—they
didn't even notice her—but by something
bigger, something she couldn't name.

When the singing ended, the pastor stood
at the front of the room and spoke about
a God who loved everyone, no matter
who they were or what they had done.
He talked about forgiveness and grace

and a love so deep it could heal even the most broken heart.

Marie didn't understand all of it, but her heart ached with something she couldn't explain. Could it be true? Could there really be someone who loved her, even her, with all her flaws and mistakes?
A Whisper in the Darkness

The days that followed were some of the hardest of Marie's young life. Her mother's anger seemed to intensify, as if that was possible....and the basement became Maries second home. She began to wonder if it would ever end, if the pain and loneliness would ever go away. She thought about ending it all, about finding a way to escape the torment forever.

It was on one of those nights, as she lay in the darkness of the basement, that she heard the voice.
"I love you. I died for you."

It was soft, like a whisper, but it was clear as day. Marie sat up, her heart racing. The dogs whined beside her, sensing her unease.
"Who's there?" she whispered, her voice trembling.

There was no answer, but the words lingered in her mind, bringing with them a strange sense of peace.

"I love you. I died for you."

Marie didn't know who had spoken those words, but something deep inside her told her they were true. For the first time, she felt the smallest flicker of hope.
She thought back to the church, to the pastor's words about a God who loved everyone. Could it be Him? Could He be the one who had spoken to her?

Marie didn't know much about God, but she made a promise to herself that night. She would go back to the church. She would find out who this God was.

Because if there was even a chance that someone loved her, truly loved her, she needed to know. Oh, how she needed to know!

CHAPTER 3: A DOOR TO HOPE

The next Sunday, Marie found herself standing outside the little church again. She hadn't planned to come back, but something about that place had stayed with her all week. It was the singing, the warmth, the way the words seemed to wrap around her like a blanket. And the whisper she had heard in the basement—those words, "I love you. I died for you,"—had echoed in her mind every night since.

She hesitated at the door, her fingers clutching the hem of her much too large dress. What if they told her to leave? What if they saw her and knew she didn't belong? She looked down at her scuffed shoes, the ones Clara had outgrown years ago and felt a pang of shame.

But then she heard the music again. It drifted out through the open doors, soft and inviting, and something inside her stirred. Taking a deep breath, and a chance she stepped inside.

The Visit

The room was just as she remembered—small and simple, with wooden pews and sunlight streaming through stained glass windows. The people were singing again, their voices filling the space with a joy that seemed almost tangible.

Marie slipped into the same pew at the back, hoping no one would notice her. She folded her hands in her lap and listened, her heart pounding, as if her heart was about to explode.
The song ended, and the pastor stepped forward. He was an older man, with kind eyes and a voice that carried both strength and gentleness. He spoke about

love that morning—about a love so great it could change lives.

"God's love," he said, "is not like the love we experience here on earth. It's not conditional. It's not something you have to earn. It's a gift, freely given to every single one of us."

Marie's brow furrowed as she tried to understand. Love that you didn't have to earn, what? That didn't make sense. In her experience, love was something you worked for, something you begged for, and even then, it could be withheld.

"God loves you just as you are," the pastor continued. "Even if you feel broken, even if you feel unworthy. He sees you, and He loves you."

Marie's chest tightened, and tears pricked at the corners of her eyes. She wanted so badly to believe those words, but a voice in the back of her mind whispered, not you. He couldn't mean you.

When the service ended, the people around her began to rise, chatting and laughing as they filed out of the pews. Marie stayed seated, unsure of what to do. She thought about leaving quietly, slipping out the door before anyone noticed her.

But then a woman approached her. She was older, with soft gray hair and a smile that crinkled the corners of her eyes.

"Hello, sweetheart," the woman said, her voice warm. "I don't think I've seen you here before. What's your name?"

Marie hesitated, glancing down at her hands. "Marie," she said softly.
"Well, Marie, I'm Mrs. Thompson. It's so nice to meet you." The woman's smile didn't waver, and for a moment, Marie felt something she hadn't felt in a long time: welcome.

The church Visits

The next Sunday, Marie woke up early. She slipped out of the house before anyone else was awake, her heart fluttering with both excitement and nerves. She didn't know why, but she was drawn to the little church. It was as if something inside her was pulling her back.

When she arrived, Mrs. Thompson was waiting for her.
"Well, hello again!" the older woman said, her smile as bright as the morning sun. "I'm so glad you came back."

Marie felt her cheeks flush as she nodded. She still wasn't used to people being kind to her, and she didn't quite know how to respond.

Mrs. Thompson led her to a seat closer to the front this time. Marie felt a little out of place, surrounded by so many people who seemed to know each other, but Mrs.

Thompson stayed by her side, introducing her to a few others and making her feel less alone.

That day, the pastor spoke about forgiveness. He talked about letting go of anger and bitterness, about how holding onto those things could weigh you down. Marie thought about her mother, about the way her anger burned like a fire that never went out. She wondered if her mother would ever let go of that anger—if she even wanted to.

But then the pastor said something that made Marie's heart skip a beat.

"Sometimes," he said, "the hardest person to forgive is yourself." What? Did I just hear that right? Marie thought. Marie froze. She hadn't realized it before, but she had been carrying her own kind of anger at herself. She blamed herself for her mother's hatred, for her father's absence, for everything that had gone wrong in her short life. Tears welled in her eyes, and she quickly wiped them away, hoping no one would notice.

Jesus

Marie began to feel like she belonged—just a little. Mrs. Thompson greeted her at the door with a hug, and a few of the other women in the congregation smiled and waved at her.

That morning, the pastor spoke about Jesus. Marie had heard His name before, but she didn't really know who He was. The pastor talked about how Jesus had lived a perfect life, how He had healed the sick and cared for the outcasts, how He had died on the cross to take away the sins of the world.

"Jesus died for you," the pastor said, looking out at the congregation. "Not because you're perfect, but because He loves you. He loves you so much, He was willing to give His life for you."
Marie felt her breath catch in her throat.

She thought about the whisper she had heard in the basement: "I love you. I died for you."
Was it Him? Was it Jesus who had spoken to her that night?
She didn't know for sure, but something inside her told her it was.

For the first time, Marie felt a glimmer of hope. It was small and fragile, like a tiny flame, but it was there.

A New Beginning

Marie didn't have all the answers yet. She still didn't fully understand who God was, or why He would love someone like her. But she kept going back to the church, week after week, drawn by the songs, the words, and the kindness of people like Mrs. Thompson.

Little by little, her heart began to open. And though her life at home hadn't changed, though her mother's anger still loomed over her like a dark cloud, Marie began to feel something she hadn't felt in a long time: hope.

Because maybe—just maybe—there was a God who loved her. And maybe that love could change everything.

CHAPTER 4: SEEDS OF FORGIVENESS

Marie's visits to the church became her lifeline. Each week, she slipped out of the house early, unnoticed, and made her way to the small white building at the end of the street. It was the only place where she felt safe, where she didn't have to tiptoe around or brace for the sting of her mother's anger.

At church, she learned about grace, love, and forgiveness—words that felt foreign and strange but also beautiful. The pastor spoke often about Jesus' love for everyone, even those who felt unlovable. He talked about how Jesus forgave the very people who hurt Him, even as He hung on the cross. Wow Marie thought!

Forgiveness.

The word lodged itself in Marie's mind, refusing to leave. She thought about her mother, about the years of bruises and harsh words. Could she forgive that? Did she even want to?

The Struggle Within

One evening, after another long day of avoiding her mother's wrath, Marie sat in her small corner of the shared bedroom she had with Clara. The house was quiet; her stepfather was working late, and her mother had finally gone to bed after yelling at her for spilling a glass of water.

Marie opened the small Bible Mrs. Thompson had given her. She couldn't read all the big words yet, but she had marked a few passages that the pastor had mentioned in his sermons. Her fingers traced over one verse in particular, the one she couldn't stop thinking about:

"Be kind to one another, tenderhearted, forgiving one another, as God in Christ forgave you." – Ephesians 4:32

Her chest tightened as she read it. Forgive her mother? How could she? Every bruise, every insult, every time she was locked in the basement came rushing back, and the thought of letting go of that pain felt impossible.

But then she thought about Jesus.

The pastor had explained how Jesus forgave the people who mocked Him, who hurt Him, who nailed Him to the cross. If He could forgive that, couldn't she forgive her mother?

Marie closed her eyes, tears streaming down her cheeks. "God," she whispered, her voice trembling, "I don't know how to do this. I don't even know if I can. But if You want me to forgive her, you're going to have to help me."

It wasn't an instant transformation.

The anger and hurt didn't disappear overnight. But something inside Marie began to shift, like a tiny crack letting in a sliver of light.

Changing the Way She Saw Her Mother

Marie began to notice things she hadn't before. She saw the deep lines etched into her mother's face, the way her shoulders sagged when she thought no one was looking. She heard the bitterness in her mother's voice, a bitterness that seemed to come from a place of pain.
And for the first time, Marie wondered if her mother was hurting, too.

The pastor often talked about how hurt people hurt others, how brokenness could spread like a disease. Marie didn't know much about her mother's past, but she had overheard bits and pieces over the years—how her mother's own father had been cruel, how she had been left to raise Clara alone after the divorced from Clara's father, then Marie's own father walked out.

Marie didn't know if those things excused her mother's behavior, but they helped her understand it.

One afternoon, when her mother was busy in the kitchen, Marie hesitated in the doorway, clutching the hem of her dress.

"Mom?" she said softly.

Her mother turned, her eyes narrowing. "What?"
"I… I just wanted to say I'm sorry. For spilling the water earlier."

Her mother blinked, clearly taken aback. She didn't respond, just turned back to the sink, muttering under her breath.

It wasn't much, but it was the first time Marie had tried to reach out to her mother, even in a small way.
Acts of Quiet Kindness

Over the weeks that followed, Marie began to do little things to show kindness to her mother. She folded the laundry, washed dishes, swept the kitchen floor, mowed the yard and even picked a handful of wildflowers from the vacant lot down the street and left them on the table.

Her mother didn't say thank you. She barely even acknowledged Marie's efforts. But Marie didn't stop.
It wasn't easy. There were still days when her mother's anger flared, when Marie found herself back in the basement, clutching the dogs for comfort. There were still nights when she cried herself to sleep, wondering if anything would ever change.
But each time she felt the bitterness creeping back in, she whispered a prayer: "God, help me forgive her. Help me love her."

A Small Moment of Breakthrough

One evening, Marie's stepfather was working late again, and Clara was out with friends. Tommy had fallen asleep early, leaving just Marie and her mother in the living room.

Marie sat at the edge of the couch, nervously twisting her hands in her lap. Her mother was flipping through a magazine, her face set in its usual scowl.

"Mom?" Marie said quietly.

Her mother didn't look up. "What?"

"I learned something at church today," Marie said, her voice trembling. "The pastor said… he said that God loves everyone. Even when they make mistakes. Even when they're hurting."

Her mother's hands froze, the magazine falling silent in her lap. She turned to look at Marie, her eyes narrowing. "What are you talking about?"

Marie swallowed hard. "I just... I thought you should know. That He loves you, too."

For a moment, her mother said nothing. Her expression was unreadable, her lips pressed into a thin line. And then she stood up abruptly, muttering something about needing to check on Tommy, and left the room.
Marie sat there, her heart pounding. She wasn't sure if she had gotten through to her mother, but something about the way her mother had looked at her—surprised, almost vulnerable—gave her hope.

The Power of Faith

Marie's faith didn't fix everything. Her mother didn't suddenly become kind and loving, and there were still days when the weight of it all felt like too much to bear. But her faith gave her strength. It gave her a way to see her mother not as a monster, but as a broken person who needed love and grace just as much as she did.

And slowly, ever so slowly, her acts of kindness began to chip away at the walls her mother had built around herself.

One morning, as Marie set the table for breakfast, her mother paused in the doorway, watching her.
"Why do you keep doing this?" her mother asked, her voice sharp but quieter than usual.

Marie looked up, her hands trembling as she placed the last plate on the table.
"Because I love you," she said simply.
Her mother's face hardened, and for a moment, Marie thought she was about to lash out. But then something in her expression shifted—just for a second—and she turned away.

Marie didn't know if her mother would ever fully change. But she knew that her own heart was changing, and that was enough to keep going.

A Journey, Not an End
Marie's relationship with her mother remained complicated, but her faith gave her the courage to keep loving, even when it was hard. She didn't know what the future held, but she held onto the hope that God was with her, guiding her every step of the way.

Because if there was one thing she had learned, it was this: love had the power to heal even the deepest wounds.

CHAPTER 5: COME AS YOU ARE

The night before, Marie thought she might die.

Her mother's rage had been worse than usual, unleashed over something insignificant—Marie couldn't even remember what it was now. She only remembered the sharp sting of the blows and the cold, hard basement floor where she had been thrown afterward. The dogs had curled up beside her as always, their warmth the only comfort she had.

She had cried herself to sleep, and when she woke the next morning, her small body ached in ways she couldn't describe. Her dress was torn at the hem, her knees scraped, and the faint metallic tang of dried blood lingered in the air.

Her reflection in the cracked basement window showed dirt streaked across her face, her hair matted and tangled.

But none of that mattered.

Because it was Sunday, and she knew she had to get to church.

The Call

Marie couldn't explain it, but she felt something deep inside her—an urgency, a pull she couldn't ignore. It was as if someone was whispering to her heart, "Come. Just come."

She didn't have time to clean up. She didn't have anything else to wear. She didn't even know if she had the strength to walk all the way to the church. But she had to go.
So, she climbed the basement steps, careful not to wake her mother, and slipped out the back door. The morning air was crisp, and the sunlight felt warm

on her bruised face. She walked slowly, her bare feet scuffing against the pavement, her torn dress fluttering in the breeze.

The closer she got to the church, the louder the pull inside her became. It was as if her heart was being drawn there, as if someone was waiting for her.

The Walk of Grace

When Marie entered the church, the service was already underway. The congregation was singing, their voices rising in harmony, and the sound washed over her like a wave.

She hesitated in the doorway, suddenly aware of how she must look. Her dress was torn, her skin bruised and dirty, and the faint smell of the basement still clung to her. She felt ashamed, unworthy. She thought about turning around and leaving, hiding herself back in the shadows where no one could see her.

But then she felt it again—that pull, that whisper.

"Come."

Something inside her told her that she didn't have to hide. That she didn't have to be perfect, or clean, or whole to be here.

So she stepped inside.

No one stared. No one whispered. No one turned her away.

Instead, Mrs. Thompson appeared at her side, her kind eyes filled with concern and love. She didn't ask questions or comment on Marie's appearance. She simply placed a hand on her shoulder and guided her to a seat.

Marie sat quietly, her hands trembling in her lap as she listened to the pastor speak. He talked about Jesus—about how He welcomed the broken, the hurting, the sinners, and the outcasts. About how His love was for everyone, no matter who they were or where they came from.

Marie thought about her own life—about the basement, the bruises, the loneliness. She thought about all the times she had felt unlovable, unworthy, unseen. And then she thought about Jesus, about the way the pastor described Him: a Savior who loved her just as she was.

The Altar Call

When the pastor invited anyone who wanted to accept Jesus into their heart to come forward, Marie didn't hesitate.

She stood up, her legs shaky but determined, and walked to the front of the church. Tears streamed down her face, cutting tracks through the dirt on her cheeks. She didn't care who saw her.

She didn't care how she looked or smelled.

All she cared about was the pull in her heart—the voice that had been calling her, drawing her here.
As she knelt at the altar, the tears came harder. She sobbed, her small frame shaking as she poured out everything—the pain, the anger, the fear, the loneliness.

"Jesus," she whispered through her tears. "I don't know why You want me. I'm dirty, and broken, and I don't have anything to give You. But if You really love me, if You really died for me… then I want to know You. I want You in my life. Please forgive me. Please help me."

She felt a hand on her shoulder, then another, then another. She looked up through her tears and saw that the congregation had surrounded her, their faces filled with love and compassion. They didn't care about her torn dress or her dirty face. They didn't care about the bruises or the smell.

They saw her the way Jesus saw her: as a child of God, precious and loved.
Mrs. Thompson knelt beside her, wrapping her arms around her in a gentle hug. "You're not alone anymore, Marie," she whispered. "You're part of His family now. And we're your family, too."

A New Beginning

When Marie left the church that morning, something felt different. The pain and bruises were still there, and she knew her life at home wouldn't change overnight. But her heart felt lighter, as if a weight she had been carrying for years had been lifted.

She didn't feel alone anymore.

For the first time, she felt loved—not because of what she had done, but because of who's she was. She was a child of God, and that was enough.

As she walked home, she whispered a quiet prayer.

"Thank You, Jesus," she said, her voice trembling. "Thank You for loving me. Thank You for finding me."

The sunlight warmed her face, and she smiled—a small, tentative smile, but a smile nonetheless.
Because she knew that no matter what happened, she was no longer walking through life alone.

A Church That Mirrors Jesus

The following weeks, the church community wrapped their arms around Marie in ways she never expected. Mrs. Thompson brought her clean clothes and helped her fix her hair. A kind couple invited her to sit with them during service, making sure she always had

someone to talk to.
No one asked too many questions about her home life, but they didn't need to. They loved her without conditions, just as Jesus did.

And little by little, Marie began to heal.

CHAPTER 6: NEVER ALONE

Marie had hoped, in those first few days after she gave her heart to Jesus, that everything would change. She had walked home from church that morning with a lightness in her step, her heart full of hope and joy. She felt as though she were carrying a secret treasure, one that no one could take away from her.

But when she stepped through the door, reality came crashing back.

Her mother's eyes narrowed the moment she saw her. "Where were you?" she demanded, her voice sharp and accusing.
Marie hesitated. "I... I went to church," she said softly.

Her mother scoffed, her lip curling in disgust. "Church? What are you playing at now? You? In church?" She let out a bitter laugh. "You think God wants anything to do with you? You're nothing but a demon child, Marie. A mistake."

The words stung, but they didn't cut as deeply as they once had. Because now, deep in her heart, Marie knew they weren't true.

She had heard another voice that day— a voice that spoke love and acceptance over her. A voice that reminded her she was wanted, chosen, and loved.

Marie didn't argue with her mother. She simply lowered her gaze and went to her room. She knelt by her bed, clasping her hands together, and whispered a prayer.

"Jesus, she still hates me. I thought You'd change her heart, but she's still so angry. Why? Why won't she stop?"

And in the quiet of her heart, she felt His

answer.
"I'm here, Marie. I'm with you. Just hold on."

Faith in the Fire

Life didn't get easier after that day. Her mother's anger didn't disappear, and the bruises didn't stop. Marie still found herself in the basement more often than not, clutching the dogs for comfort as tears streamed down her face.

But something was different now.

She no longer felt the crushing weight of hopelessness. The thought of ending her life, which had haunted her so many times before, never returned. Because now she had a Friend—a real Friend—who was with her every step of the way. When her mother called her a demon, Marie whispered to herself, "Jesus says I'm His child."

When her mother's hand struck her,

Marie prayed, "Jesus, help me forgive her."

When the darkness of the basement closed in around her, Marie closed her eyes and imagined Jesus sitting beside her, His arms wrapped around her, whispering, "You are loved. You are not alone."

And when the pain became too much to bear, she poured out her heart to Him, questioning, crying, and sometimes even yelling.
"Why don't You stop her, Jesus?" she asked one night, her voice breaking. "You're God. You can do anything. Why do You let her hurt me?"

She didn't always get the answers she wanted, but she always felt His presence, steady and unshakable.

"Even I couldn't please everyone, Marie," He reminded her gently. "Even I was betrayed, hurt, and rejected. This world isn't perfect because of sin. But I'm with you. Always. I will never leave you my child"

Learning to Trust
Marie's faith didn't come without struggles. There were days when she doubted, when she questioned whether God really cared about her.

"Why me?" she asked one afternoon, sitting on the steps of the church after Sunday service. Mrs. Thompson had invited her to stay for lunch, but Marie had needed a moment alone to think.

"Why did You let me be born into this family? Why do Clara and Tommy get love, and I get... this?"
The breeze stirred her hair, and she closed her eyes, waiting for an answer. And then she remembered something the pastor had said during his sermon that morning:

"God never promised us a life without

pain, but He promised to walk with us through it. He promised to use even our hardest moments for good, if we trust Him."

Marie didn't understand how her pain could ever be used for good. But she clung to the promise that God was with her, that He saw her tears and heard her prayers.

A Friend Who Never Leaves

It was this growing faith, this quiet assurance, that gave Marie the strength to keep going.
When her mother's insults tried to burrow into her heart, she reminded herself of what Jesus had said: "You are precious to Me."

When the bruises ached and the darkness of the basement felt overwhelming, she sang softly to herself the songs she had learned in church.

"Amazing grace, how sweet the sound…"

Sometimes, late at night, she would imagine Jesus sitting beside her, His hand resting on hers. She would talk to Him, telling Him about her day, her fears, her hopes. And even though she couldn't see Him, she felt His presence, as real as the dogs curled up by her side. "You're my best friend," she whispered one night, tears streaming down her face. "Thank You for staying with me."

Faith in the Questions
Marie's faith didn't stop her from asking hard questions.

"Why did You let my father leave?"

"Why don't You make my mother stop hurting me?"
"Why do You love me, when I'm so… broken?"
And every time, Jesus met her with the same quiet, steady love.

"I love you because you're Mine."

"I'm with you, even in the pain."

"Trust Me, Marie. I have a plan for you."

There were days when those answers didn't feel like enough. Days when Marie's heart ached with the weight of it all. But she kept coming back to Jesus, again and again, because she knew He was the only one who truly understood her pain.

A Light in the Darkness

Marie's life didn't become perfect after she gave her heart to Jesus. Her mother's anger didn't vanish, and the bruises didn't fade overnight. But her heart was no longer weighed down by hopelessness.

She had found a Friend who walked with her through every dark moment, who reminded her that she was loved, cherished, and never alone.

And though her questions remained, her faith grew stronger with each passing day.

Because now, no matter what her mother said or did, Marie knew the truth:
She was not a demon.

She was not a mistake.

She was a child of God.

And that truth was enough to carry her through even the darkest of days.

CHAPTER 7: THE BREAKING POINT

The signs had been there for weeks—Marie's growing fatigue, the way her arms and legs ached more than usual, the dizziness that left her clutching walls for balance. But in her world, pain was a constant companion, and she had learned to push through it as best she could. After all, showing weakness at home only invited more trouble.

Her mother didn't notice. Or if she did, she didn't care.

"You're always whining about something," her mother snapped one evening as Marie swayed on her feet while washing the dishes. "Stop looking for attention and finish your chores."

Marie bit her lip, forcing herself to stay upright as her vision blurred. She didn't dare sit down until the last dish was scrubbed and dried.

School Days, Hunger Pains

At school, things weren't much better. Her mother rarely gave her lunch money, and Marie often went the entire day without eating. She could feel the stares of her classmates as her stomach growled during lessons, but she kept her head down, too ashamed to meet their eyes.

One day, her teacher, Mrs. Whitaker, pulled her aside after class.

"Marie, are you feeling all right?" she asked, her kind eyes scanning Marie's pale face.

Marie hesitated, clutching her worn backpack tightly. "I'm fine," she muttered.
Mrs. Whitaker frowned, kneeling to meet her gaze. "You don't look fine, sweetheart. Are you eating enough at home?"

Marie's heart raced. She thought about telling the truth—about the hunger that gnawed at her stomach, about the nights spent locked in the basement—but fear silenced her. What if her mother found out she had said something?

"I'm fine," she repeated, her voice barely above a whisper.

Mrs. Whitaker sighed, clearly unconvinced, but she didn't press further.

The Collapse

The breaking point came one chilly afternoon during recess. Marie had been sitting on a bench, too tired to play with the other kids, when one of her classmates called out to her.
"Hey, Marie! Come play tag with us!"
Before she could answer, the world around her tilted. Her vision darkened, and the next thing she knew, she was lying on the ground, a circle of

concerned faces looming over her.

"She fainted!" someone whispered.

"Go get the teacher!"

When she came to, she was in the nurse's office, her head pounding and her body trembling. The school nurse frowned as she took Marie's pulse, her expression a mix of worry and confusion.

"Marie, when's the last time you ate?" the nurse asked gently.
Marie blinked, trying to remember. Was it yesterday? The day before? She wasn't sure.
"I don't know," she mumbled.
The nurse exchanged a look with Mrs. Whitaker, who had come rushing in after hearing what happened.
"We're calling an ambulance," the nurse said firmly.

The Hospital

The hospital smelled of antiseptic and something faintly metallic, a sharp contrast to the damp, musty air of Marie's basement. She lay on a narrow bed, her small frame dwarfed by the oversized hospital gown. Nurses moved around her, taking blood samples and checking her vitals.

"Do you feel dizzy often?" one of them asked.

Marie nodded weakly.

"Do you bruise easily?"

She hesitated, glancing at the mottled patches on her arms and legs.

"Yes." Marie was scared she didn't want to get her mom into trouble and she sure didn't want her mom mad at her that never went over well, not in her favor. She didn't want to lie so she was as careful as possible.

The nurses exchanged concerned glances before leaving the room to speak with the doctor.

Her Mother's Visit

When her mother arrived, her face was a mask of false concern. She swept into the room, her voice dripping with exaggerated sweetness as she spoke to the doctor.

"She's always been a bit clumsy," her mother said, shaking her head with a sigh. "She gets it from her father, I think. Always tripping over her own feet. And she's such a picky eater! I've tried everything to get her to eat more, but you know how kids are."

The doctor nodded, taking notes. "We're running some tests to rule out anemia or a bleeding disorder," he said. "Her bruising and fatigue are concerning."

Marie's mother put on her best worried-parent expression. "Oh, I hope it's nothing serious. She's my baby—I don't know what I'd do if something happened to her."

Marie stared at the ceiling, her heart sinking. She knew no one would see through her mother's act. No one ever did.

When the doctor and nurses left the room, her mother's demeanor changed instantly.

"You'd better not embarrass me," she hissed, her eyes cold and sharp. "Keep your mouth shut about what happens at home. Do you hear me?" "Or you know it will be all your fault when they send you to someone that don't care nothing about you. You think you're so special, but you are nothing so stop trying to get attention. These doctors and nurses have children with real problems and here you are taking up all there valuable time. Understand me?"

Marie nodded silently, clutching the thin

hospital blanket.

A Whisper in the Darkness

That night, as the hospital grew quiet, Marie lay awake, staring at the faint glow of the clock on the wall. She felt small and alone, the weight of everything pressing down on her chest.

"Jesus," she whispered, her voice trembling. "Why does it have to be like this? Why won't You stop her?"
Tears slipped down her cheeks, soaking the pillow beneath her head. She thought back to the verse Mrs. Thompson had shared with her:
"The Lord is close to the brokenhearted and saves those who are crushed in spirit." – Psalm 34:18
"Are You here?" she asked softly. "Do You see me?"
In the stillness, she felt a quiet peace settle over her heart, like a gentle whisper:
I see you, Marie. I'm with you.

The words didn't erase the pain or the fear, but they gave her something to hold onto—a lifeline in the darkness.

The Test Results

The next morning, the doctor returned with the test results.

"The good news is, it's not leukemia," he said, offering a reassuring smile. "But Marie is severely malnourished, and her iron levels are dangerously low. That's why she's been so tired and bruises so easily."

Her mother nodded; her face carefully composed. "I'll make sure she eats better," she said sweetly.

Marie didn't believe her. But she kept her mouth shut like her mom had instructed.

Returning Home

When Marie was discharged, her

mother's anger simmered just beneath the surface.

"You're lucky they didn't keep you longer," she snapped as they walked into the house. "You've caused me enough trouble already."

Marie said nothing, retreating to her room and closing the door behind her. She knelt by her bed, clutching her Bible to her chest.

"Jesus, I don't know what to do," she whispered. "But I trust You. Please help me."

A Glimmer of Hope

Despite everything, Marie's faith remained steadfast. She continued going to church whenever she could, leaning on the kindness of Mrs. Thompson and the pastor for support.

One Sunday, as she sat in the pew listening to the sermon, she felt a familiar pull in her heart—the same pull that had led her to the church in the first place.

It wasn't a voice, exactly, but a quiet certainty, like a hand gently guiding her.

"I have plans for you, Marie," the pastor read from Jeremiah 29:11. "Plans to prosper you and not to harm you, plans to give you hope and a future."

Marie closed her eyes, letting the words wash over her. She didn't know what the future held, but she knew one thing for certain: she wasn't alone. Marie's journey was far from over, but she had found something stronger than fear, stronger than pain.
She had found hope.
And that hope would carry her through whatever came next.

Chapter 8: Strength in the Storm

Marie had always thought of her mother's anger as a storm—a force of nature that swept through their house, unpredictable and relentless. She had learned to survive it by staying quiet, by making herself small, by hiding in the shadows. But now, as she sat on the cold basement floor with the dogs pressed close to her sides, she realized something had changed.

The storm still raged, but it no longer had the power to destroy her.

Her mother's words echoed in her mind—sharp, cutting, meant to wound. "You're useless, Marie. Worthless. You'll never be anything."
For years, those words had burrowed deep into her heart, leaving scars she thought would never heal. But now, another voice whispered over them,

drowning them out with a quiet, steady truth: "You are Mine."

Marie closed her eyes, clutching her small Bible to her chest. She didn't understand why her mother hated her so much, why the bruises and the insults never stopped. But she knew this: she wasn't alone.

The Power of Forgiveness

At church, Pastor James often talked about forgiveness. He said it wasn't easy, that it was one of the hardest things God asked us to do. But he also said it was necessary—not for the person who had hurt you, but for yourself.

"Forgiveness doesn't mean what they did was okay," he had said during a sermon. "It doesn't mean you forget the pain they caused. It means you let go of the anger and bitterness that's weighing you down. It means you trust God to handle it."

Marie thought about those words often, especially on nights like this when the weight of her mother's hatred threatened to crush her.

"Jesus," she whispered into the darkness, her voice trembling, "I want to forgive her. I don't know how, but I want to. Please help me."

She didn't feel any different after praying. The anger and hurt didn't magically disappear. But she kept praying, night after night, asking God to soften her heart.

And slowly, she began to see her mother differently.

Seeing Her Mother Through God's Eyes

Marie started to notice things she hadn't before—the deep lines etched into her mother's face, the way her hands shook when she thought no one was looking, the weariness in her eyes that even anger couldn't hide.

She remembered something Pastor James had said: "Hurt people hurt people." Was her mother hurting, too?

Marie didn't know much about her mother's past, but she had overheard bits and pieces over the years. She knew her mother had grown up in a strict, unkind household. She knew her father had left when she was young, and her first husband—Marie's father—had walked out on her, too.

Marie didn't know if those things excused her mother's behavior, but they helped her understand it. Her mother was broken, just like her.

And maybe, just maybe, she needed love as much as Marie did.
A Small Act of Kindness

One afternoon, Marie stood in the kitchen, staring at the pile of dishes in the sink. Her mother was sitting in the living room, flipping through a magazine, her face set in its usual scowl.

Marie hesitated, clutching the hem of her too-large dress. She wanted to do something kind for her mother, even if it wasn't noticed or appreciated.

Taking a deep breath, she rolled up her sleeves and began washing the dishes. The warm water stung her bruised hands, but she kept going, scrubbing each plate until it gleamed.

When she finished, she dried her hands and stepped into the living room.

"Mom?" she said softly.

Her mother glanced at her, her eyes narrowing. "What?"

"I... I did the dishes," Marie said, her voice trembling. "I just thought it might help."

Her mother stared at her for a long

moment, her expression unreadable. Then she turned back to her magazine.

"About time you did something useful," she muttered.

Marie's heart sank, but she whispered a prayer under her breath: "Jesus, help me love her anyway."

Clinging to Scripture
Marie's Bible became her lifeline during the hardest days. She carried it with her everywhere, flipping through its pages whenever she had a quiet moment.

One of her favorite verses was from 2 Corinthians 12:9:

"But He said to me, 'My grace is sufficient for you, for My power is made perfect in weakness.' Therefore, I will boast all the more gladly about my weaknesses, so that Christ's power may rest on me."

The words reminded her that she didn't

have to be strong on her own. God's strength was enough to carry her through, even when she felt like she couldn't take another step.

Another verse she clung to was Romans 8:28:
"And we know that in all things God works for the good of those who love Him, who have been called according to His purpose."

Marie didn't understand how God could use her pain for good, but she trusted that He had a plan.
A Moment of Grace

One evening, as Marie sat at the kitchen table doing her homework, her mother walked in, muttering under her breath about something that had gone wrong at work.
Marie hesitated, then said softly, "Mom, is there anything I can do to help?"
Her mother froze, her eyes narrowing.
"Why are you asking?" she snapped.

"I just… thought maybe you could use some help," Marie said, keeping her gaze fixed on the table.

Her mother didn't respond right away. Instead, she stood there, staring at Marie with an expression that was almost… confused.

Finally, she shook her head and walked away, muttering, "Ridiculous."

But for a moment, Marie thought she saw something in her mother's eyes—a flicker of something softer, something almost vulnerable.

Marie whispered a prayer as her mother left the room: "Jesus, please help her. Please show her that You love her."

The Strength to Keep Going

Marie's relationship with her mother didn't change overnight. The anger and the bruises didn't magically disappear. But Marie's faith gave her the strength to keep going.

She learned to see her mother not as a monster, but as a broken person in need of God's grace. She learned to forgive, even when it was hard. And she learned to trust that God was with her, even in the darkest moments.

One night, as she lay in bed, she whispered a quiet prayer:

"Thank You, Jesus, for loving me. And thank You for loving her, too. Please help me keep going. Please help me be kind, even when it's hard. I don't know what You're doing, but I trust You."
And as she drifted off to sleep, she felt a peace settle over her—a peace that came from knowing she was held in the arms of a God who would never let her go.

"The Lord is my strength and my shield; my heart trusts in Him, and He helps me.

My heart leaps for joy, and with my song I praise Him." – Psalm 28:7

Chapter 9: A Birthday Wish

The days leading up to Marie's eighth birthday passed like any other. There were no mentions of celebrations, no presents hidden away in her mother's closet, and certainly no talk of cake or candles. Marie had learned long ago not to expect such things. Her birthdays were just another day on the calendar, forgotten like so many others.

However, this year felt different somehow!

As her birthday approached, Marie felt a pull in her heart—stronger than anything she had ever felt before. It was the same pull that had led her to the small white church months ago, the same whisper that had called out to her in the darkness: "I love you. I died for you."

This time, the whisper carried a new message.

"Be baptized."

Marie didn't fully understand why it felt so urgent, but she knew one thing for certain: Jesus was calling her to take this step, and she had to obey. She honestly wasn't sure what baptism was, but she felt she needed it and now no waiting allowed, but why?
The Conversation

One Sunday after service, Marie waited near the front of the church as the congregation filed out. She clutched her Bible tightly, her small hands trembling as she rehearsed the words in her mind. Pastor James and his wife, Mrs. Emily, were standing by the altar, chatting with a few members of the congregation.

When the others left, Marie stepped forward, her heart pounding in her chest.

"Pastor James?" she said softly.

The pastor turned, his kind eyes lighting up when he saw her. "Marie! How are you, sweetheart?"

"I… I need to talk to you," she said, her voice trembling.

"Of course," he said, kneeling to her level. "What's on your mind?"

Mrs. Emily joined them, her warm smile reassuring Marie as she hesitated.

"It's about my birthday," Marie began, her fingers gripping the edges of her Bible. "I'm going to be eight soon."

"That's wonderful!" Mrs. Emily said. "Do you have anything special planned?" Marie shook her head. "I've never had a party or a cake or anything like that. But… I don't really want those things."

Pastor James tilted his head, studying

her with gentle curiosity. "What do you want, then?"

Marie took a deep breath, her eyes filling with tears. "I want to be baptized. Jesus says I need to do this, and I need to do it now. I don't know why, but I feel like it's the only thing I should do for my birthday. It's all I want. Please, Pastor James. I must obey Him."

The pastor's eyes softened, and Mrs. Emily reached out to place a comforting hand on Marie's shoulder.

"Marie," Pastor James said, his voice steady and kind, "baptism is a beautiful step of faith. It's a way to tell the world that you belong to Jesus, that you've given your heart to Him."

Marie nodded quickly. "I know. And I have. I gave my heart to Him a long time ago. But now... now I need to show it. I need to tell everyone. Even my mom, even if she gets mad. I have to do this."

Pastor James exchanged a glance with Mrs. Emily, who smiled and nodded.

"Then we'll make it happen," he said firmly. "We'll plan your baptism for your birthday."

Marie's eyes widened. "Really? Even if my mom says no?"

Pastor James hesitated, his brow furrowing. "We'll pray about that, Marie. God will make a way. If this is something He's calling you to do, nothing will stop it."

Breaking the News at Home

That evening, Marie sat at the kitchen table, nervously tapping her fingers against the wood. Her mother was in the living room, flipping through a magazine, and Marie knew this wasn't the best time to talk to her. But she also knew there would never be a "good" time.

Taking a deep breath, she stood and walked into the living room.

"Mom?" she said softly.

Her mother didn't look up. "What?"
"I... I need to tell you something."

Her mother sighed, tossing the magazine aside. "What is it, Marie? I don't have all day."

Marie clasped her hands together, her heart pounding. "My birthday is coming up, and... and the only thing I want is to be baptized."
Her mother frowned, her lips tightening into a thin line. "Baptized? What are you talking about?"

"At church," Marie said quickly, her words tumbling out in a rush. "They said I can do it on my birthday. It's all I want, Mom. I don't need a party or a cake or anything like that. I just need to do this."

Her mother's eyes narrowed. "You've been spending too much time at that church," she said, her voice icy. "I knew it would put crazy ideas in your head."

"It's not crazy," Marie said, her voice trembling. "Jesus is calling me to do this. I have to obey Him."

Her mother laughed bitterly. "Jesus? You think He cares about you? You think He's going to fix everything with a little dunk in some water?"

Marie bit her lip, fighting back tears. "It's not about fixing things," she said quietly. "It's about showing Him that I love Him. That I belong to Him."

Her mother stood abruptly, towering over her. "You're not doing this, Marie. I won't have people thinking I can't control my own kid. You're not embarrassing me in front of that church."

Marie's heart sank, but she stood her ground. "I'm going to do it," she said softly but firmly. "Even if you say no. I have to."

Her mother's face darkened, and for a moment, Marie thought she might lash out. But instead, she simply turned and walked away, muttering under her breath.

The Day of the Baptism

When Marie arrived at church on her birthday, her heart was heavy with nerves but also filled with a quiet determination. Her mother hadn't said a word to her that morning, pretending as if it were just another day. But Marie didn't let it stop her.

Mrs. Thompson greeted her at the door, pulling her into a warm hug. "Happy birthday, sweetheart," she said, her eyes shining with pride. "Are you ready?"

Marie nodded, clutching her Bible tightly. "I'm ready."

The service was simple but beautiful. As the congregation sang a hymn, Marie stepped into the baptismal pool, her small frame trembling with both fear and excitement. Pastor James stood beside her, his hands steady as he smiled down at her.

"Marie," he said, his voice warm, "have you accepted Jesus as your Lord and Savior?"

"Yes," Marie said, her voice strong and clear.

"Do you promise to follow Him all the days of your life?"

"I do."
"Then it is my honor to baptize you in the name of the Father, the Son, and the Holy Spirit".

As Pastor James lowered her into the water, Marie felt a peace wash over her like she had never known. When she came up, the congregation erupted into applause, their faces filled with joy.

Mrs. Emily wrapped her in a towel as she stepped out of the pool, whispering, "You're so brave, Marie. Jesus is so proud of you."

Marie smiled; her heart swollen with a joy she couldn't put into words.

A New Beginning
That night, as she lay in bed, Marie whispered a quiet prayer.

"Thank You, Jesus, for letting me do this. Thank You for loving me, even when it's hard. Please help me keep following You, no matter what."

And as she drifted off to sleep, she felt the same whisper in her heart that had called her to the church so many months ago:

"You are Mine."

"Therefore, if anyone is in Christ, the new creation has come: The old has gone, the new is here!" – 2 Corinthians 5:17

Chapter 10: An Overcomer in Faith

Marie's home life was far from perfect—oh, painfully far—but something remarkable had shifted within her heart. Though the beatings didn't stop, and her mother's anger still lashed out in harsh words, Marie had found something greater than herself to lean on. She no longer felt entirely alone, no longer crushed beneath the weight of fear and hopelessness. For now, she believed with all her heart that no matter what happened, she belonged to Jesus. And in belonging to Him, she found courage she'd never known before.

Her fears—of death, of her mother, of a life filled with nothing but suffering—didn't disappear overnight, but they loosened their grip on her spirit. When fear whispered lies in her mind, she clung to the promise of Scripture: "For God has not given us a spirit of fear, but of power and of love and of a sound mind" (2 Timothy 1:7). These words became her anchor. She repeated them in her prayers at night, letting them sink into her soul. Slowly but surely, her fear began to fade, replaced by the quiet assurance that God was her protector.

"The Lord is my light and my salvation—whom shall I fear? The Lord is the stronghold of my life—of whom shall I be afraid?" (Psalm 27:1).

Even as the bruises on her body lingered and the pain of her mother's rejection stung her heart, Marie realized she didn't have to face her suffering alone. Her prayers became her refuge. In the darkest moments, she leaned on the strength of Christ, whispering to her,
"I can do all things through Christ who strengthens me" (Philippians 4:13).
No longer did she carry her burdens in silence; she had faith to shoulder the weight. She believed that even if her trials didn't end, they would make her stronger, just as God's Word promised:

"Blessed is the one who perseveres under trial because, having stood the test, that person will receive the crown of life that the Lord has promised to those who love him" (James 1:12).

The church, too, became a sanctuary for Marie—a place of hope and healing in a world that often felt cruel and unforgiving. Remarkably, her mother never tried to stop her from attending church or participating in its functions. Perhaps it was indifference, or perhaps, deep down, her mother saw that those moments of peace were what kept Marie going. Whatever the reason, the church welcomed her with open arms, wrapping her in a love she had never known at home.

When it came to retreats, youth events, or other church functions, Marie never had to worry about money. The congregation always found a way to cover the costs, ensuring she could participate without her mother having the chance to say no. Their generosity extended beyond church activities—Marie even began eating at least one meal a day because of a mysterious blessing. Each week, a paid meal ticket would quietly find its way to her, allowing her to eat at school. This was long before free meal programs existed, and she never learned who was behind the kindness. But in her heart, she knew it was God providing for her needs, just as He promised in His Word:

"And my God will meet all your needs according to the riches of his glory in Christ Jesus" (Philippians 4:19).

The church community lived out the command of Scripture: "Carry each other's burdens, and in this way you will fulfill the law of Christ" (Galatians 6:2). They lifted Marie when she couldn't stand on her own, showing her that she was not forgotten. Their kindness and care taught her that God's love could shine through even the most ordinary acts of generosity.

Though her life was still far from easy,

Marie's faith gave her something she had never known before, hope. She clung to the promise of Jeremiah 29:11 "For I know the plans I have for you," declares the Lord, "plans to prosper you and not to harm you, plans to give you hope and a future." These words reminded her that her suffering wasn't the end of her story—that God had a plan for her life, even if she couldn't see it yet. She held tightly to the truth of Psalm 34:18: "The Lord is close to the brokenhearted and saves those who are crushed in spirit." In her darkest moments, she believed that God was near, that He saw her pain, and that He cared for her.

Through her faith, Marie became an overcomer. She didn't let her mother's abuse define her, nor did she allow her circumstances to steal her joy. Instead, she chose to anchor herself in God's promises and the kindness of those around her. She embraced the truth of Romans 12:21: "Do not be overcome by evil but overcome evil with good." And she trusted the words of Romans 8:37: "No, in all these things we are more than conquerors through him who loved us." Marie's victory wasn't in the changing of her circumstances, but in the transformation of her heart. She became a conqueror not because her life was easy, but because her faith gave her the strength to rise above her pain.

As she grew in her faith, Marie found peace in knowing that God's love would sustain her through every trial. Her life was still imperfect, and her struggles remained, but she no longer faced them alone. She had hope. She had courage. And she had the unshakable belief that she belonged to a God who loved her deeply and eternally.

Marie's story is one of triumph—not because her life became perfect, but because her faith made her victorious. She was an overcomer, not by her own strength, but by the strength of the One who carried her through. And sometimes, that's the greatest miracle of all.

Not the end............ only the beginning really

Epilogue: A Hope That Grows

Marie stood outside the little white church, her fingers brushing against the pages of her well-worn Bible. The morning light filtered through the trees, casting shadows on the overgrown grass. At thirteen, she was taller now, her frame still small but stronger than it had been in the years when hunger and heartbreak weighed her down.

It had been nearly 6 years since she'd first walked through the doors of this sanctuary. Five years since she'd knelt at the altar with tear-streaked cheeks and a shattered heart, giving her life to Jesus. And though her journey since then hadn't been easy, Marie could see how much had changed—not just in her, but in the world around her.

A Glimmer of Change at Home

Home was still a place of tension. Her

mother's anger hadn't disappeared, but it had softened around the edges, like the embers of a fire that no longer burned as hot. There were fewer bruises now, though the sharp words still came too often. Yet there were moments small, fleeting moments that gave Marie hope.

One such moment had come just a few weeks ago. It was a quiet evening, the kind that rarely happened in their house. Her mother had been sitting at the kitchen table, staring into her coffee cup, the lines on her face deeper than ever. Marie had hesitated in the doorway, clutching the hem of her shirt.

She said softly.

Her mother glanced up; her expression guarded. "What?"
"I just wanted to say… I'm praying for you," Marie said, her voice trembling.
Her mother's eyes narrowed, but she didn't respond right away. For a moment, Marie thought she'd made a

mistake. But then her mother sighed, a sound that was more weary than angry.

"Do whatever you want," she muttered, her voice lacking its usual bite.

It wasn't much, but it was something. And for Marie, that was enough.

A Growing Faith

At church, Marie had become more than just the quiet girl in the back pew. She was part of the youth group now, a small but lively group of teenagers who met every Wednesday evening to pray, share their struggles, and encourage one another. For the first time in her life, Marie had friends, real friends, who cared about her, who saw her for who she was, not for the bruises she hid beneath her sleeves.

Mrs. Thompson, who had been like a grandmother to her, often joined their youth group meetings, her gentle wisdom guiding the conversations.

"Marie," she'd said one evening, after a particularly emotional prayer session, "you have a gift. Your faith—it's strong, stronger than many adults I know. Don't ever let anyone take that from you, sweetheart."

Marie had smiled, her heart swelling with gratitude. She didn't feel strong most days, but she trusted that God was working through her, even when she couldn't see it.

A New Role at Church

As the years passed, Marie began to take on small roles in the church. She helped Mrs. Emily set up for Sunday school, folding chairs and organizing lesson materials. Sometimes, Pastor James asked her to read a Bible verse during the service, her voice steady despite the nerves that fluttered in her chest.

One Sunday, Pastor James approached her after the service, a thoughtful expression on his face.

"Marie," he said, "I've been praying about this, and I feel like God is calling you to share your testimony with the youth group. Would you be willing to do that?"

Marie's eyes widened. "My testimony?"

"Yes," he said with a nod. "Your story is powerful, Marie. You've been through so much, and yet your faith has remained unshaken. I think the other kids need to hear that—to see that God's love is bigger than any pain they might be feeling."

Marie hesitated, her fingers tightening around her Bible. The thought of standing in front of her peers, bearing her soul, was terrifying. But then she remembered the whisper she had heard all those years ago:

"I love you. I died for you."

If Jesus had been willing to give everything for her, how could she say no to sharing what He'd done in her life?

The Night of the Testimony

The youth group meeting was smaller than usual that night, which eased Marie's nerves slightly. She sat in a circle with the other teens, her Bible resting on her lap. When Pastor James nodded at her, she took a deep breath and began.

"My name is Marie," she said, her voice shaking slightly. "And I want to tell you about how Jesus saved me."

She spoke softly at first, her words hesitant as she described her childhood, the bruises, the basement, the loneliness. But as she continued, her voice grew steadier, filled with the quiet strength that came from knowing she wasn't telling her story alone.

She talked about the first time she walked into the church, about the kindness of Mrs. Thompson and the words of Pastor James. She described the night she heard the whisper in the basement, and the day of her baptism, and the countless ways God had carried her through every storm since then.

"And even though my life isn't perfect," she said, her voice trembling with emotion, "I know that I'm not alone. Jesus is with me every step of the way. And if He can love someone like me, He can love anyone."

When she finished, the room was silent. Tears glistened in the eyes of some of her peers, and even Pastor James looked moved.

"Thank you, Marie," he said, his voice full of warmth. "Your faith is a testament to God's power and love."

Looking Forward

As Marie walked home that night, the cool evening air brushing against her face, she felt a quiet sense of peace. Her life was still far from easy—her mother's anger flared up often, and the wounds of her past sometimes felt too heavy to bear. But she had hope, and she had faith, and she knew that was enough.

In the years to come, Marie would continue to grow in her faith. She would face new challenges, new heartbreaks, and new joys. But she would always carry with her the lessons she had learned in those early years—that God's love was bigger than her pain, that forgiveness was a gift she could give herself, and that she was never alone.

As she reached the front steps of her house, Marie paused and looked up at the night sky. The stars seemed to shine brighter than usual, their light cutting through the darkness.

"Thank You, Jesus," she whispered. "For everything."
And in her heart, she felt the same gentle whisper she had heard all those years ago:
"You are Mine."

"Let no man despise you for your youth, but be thou an example in word, in conversation, in charity, in spirit, in faith, in purity."
1 Timothy 4:12

OTHER STORIES BY MM MYERS

LOVE & TRUTH

www.ingramcontent.com/pod-product-compliance
Lightning Source LLC
Chambersburg PA
CBHW061107100726

47911CB00012B/434